The Meadow Vale Ponies

MULBERRY

TO THE RESCUE!

ALSO AVAILABLE:

Mulberry and the Summer Show

Mulberry for Sale

COMING SOON:

Mulberry Gets up to Mischief

MULBERRY
TO THE
RESCUE!

Che Golden

OXFORD
UNIVERSITY PRESS

OXFORD
UNIVERSITY PRESS

Great Clarendon Street, Oxford OX2 6DP
Oxford University Press is a department of the University of Oxford.
It furthers the University's objective of excellence in research, scholarship,
and education by publishing worldwide in

Oxford New York

Auckland Cape Town Dar es Salaam Hong Kong Karachi
Kuala Lumpur Madrid Melbourne Mexico City Nairobi
New Delhi Shanghai Taipei Toronto

With offices in

Argentina Austria Brazil Chile Czech Republic France Greece
Guatemala Hungary Italy Japan Poland Portugal Singapore
South Korea Switzerland Thailand Turkey Ukraine Vietnam

Oxford is a registered trade mark of Oxford University Press
in the UK and in certain other countries

British Library Cataloguing in Publication Data

Data available

ISBN: 978-0-19-273470-9

1 3 5 7 9 10 8 6 4 2

Printed in Great Britain

Paper used in the production of this book is a natural,
recyclable product made from wood grown in sustainable forests.
The manufacturing process conforms to the environmental
regulations of the country of origin.

For Paul, who puts

up with the menagerie

Chapter 1

Mulberry was having a lovely dream. Afterwards she couldn't remember what it was about exactly but she knew green apples were involved. So she wasn't best pleased when a noise outside her stable woke her up. Mulberry was very, very bad-tempered and waking up from a dream about juicy, tart, green apples wasn't going to improve her mood. She cracked open one eyelid and glared at the door. It was still dark outside, which meant it wasn't time for breakfast. Whoever had dared to wake her up was going to get either a bite or a kick—maybe both if she was quick enough.

But what was that smell? She flared her nostrils to take in great gulps of air and pricked her ears  eagerly. Pony nuts, if she wasn't mistaken— grass dried and rolled into pellets to make them delicious and nutritious. She licked her lips. Mulberry tended to put on weight easily and the child she owned, Sam, didn't give her much hard feed, just lots of fresh grass and hay nets. So hard feed was a real treat.

A shape appeared at the door and rattled a feed bucket gently at her. 'There's a good girl,' said a man's voice. 'Do you want some of this?'

Mulberry ignored him—Sam was the only human who actually listened to ponies when they talked, so she knew this man was just making noise for the sake of it—but she stepped forward and stretched out her neck, lips snapping at the air as she imagined the taste of those lovely rich pony nuts in her mouth. The bolt on her door was being drawn back quietly until the stable door swung open, letting in a breath of cool night air.

'Good girl, on you come now,' whispered the man. He was walking backwards and dropping the pony nuts on the ground, which annoyed Mulberry. Why couldn't he stand still and just let her stick her head in the bucket and gobble them all up?

Two-legs could always find new ways of being awkward. But pony nuts were pony nuts no matter what way she got them, so Mulberry bent her head, stretched out her lips, and snaffled the nuts up one by one, stepping forward slowly as she followed the trail.

She did get a little suspicious when they reached the car park and the trail of nuts led her onto the ramp of a horse lorry. She looked around and glared when she heard her hoof beats ring hollow and saw the thin metal bend slightly beneath her weight. But the man carried on making soothing noises and, more importantly, he kept dropping the pony nuts, so she kept walking. Besides, she could smell familiar horses in front of her.

She gave a whinny of delight when the

man finally stopped and hung the bucket up, letting her bury her nose in all those treats. She didn't even feel it when he tied a head collar around her face and clipped the lead rope to the side of the trailer. She only realized something was wrong when

an engine rumbled into life and the lorry started to sway as it drove away from the yard.

She looked at the other two horses tied up in the lorry with her.

'We're being nicked, aren't we?' she asked.

Velvet and Lucy looked back at her with terrified eyes and nodded.

Mulberry sighed. 'I knew all this hard feed was too good to be true.'

Chapter 2

Sam felt as if her world had ended. She couldn't think, she couldn't speak, she couldn't even cry, though her eyeballs were hot and itchy with unshed tears. She could only hold onto the open stable door to stop herself from falling to the ground as she stared at Mulberry's empty stable. It smelled of her pony, and a few wisps of uneaten hay lay on the ground beneath the sagging hay net. Sam just could not believe that Mulberry wasn't there, larger than life, either whinnying with joy that Sam was turning up with breakfast or complaining about the room service.

Sam turned away and began to walk with feet of lead through the yard and to the office, where the police were interviewing her mother and Janey, one of the yard's riding instructors and the owner of Lucy. The yard was hushed and still and no one, liveries nor staff, spoke to her as she dragged herself past them. A few people gave her sympathetic smiles but she saw in their faces that they didn't know what to say. What could be said?

In the office, Miss Mildew, the owner of Meadow Vale Riding School, was giving a statement to two police officers, all of them gathered around a table, hot drinks steaming in front of them, untouched. Janey sat with her face buried in her hands, her body shuddering as she sobbed. Mum sat white-faced, listening to Miss Mildew,

while Sam's big sister Amy held Sam's hand under the table.

'They cut the chains that tied up the yard gates but there were no tyre tracks on the yard itself,' Miss Mildew said. 'They must have left the lorry on the road and led the horses down through the yard. They even stole the head collars!'

'Why those three?' Mum asked. 'Of all the horses and ponies on this yard, why take Velvet, Lucy, and Mulberry?'

One of the officers checked his notes. 'Probably for their colour and their breed, I'm afraid,' he said. 'Pure cobs and cob crosses like Velvet and Lucy will always have a market, and lots of people like a native pony for their children. Black is a popular colour—a glossy black horse will sell quickly—and black and white is fashionable at the moment, unfortunately for Lucy. Everyone wants a gypsy horse.'

'What are the chances of getting them back?' Mum asked, her voice shaking as she swallowed a hard lump of tears.

The police officer went a bit pink and stared hard at his notes, while the other coughed nervously.

'To be honest, it can be very hard to get them back,' he said. He looked terrified as

Janey began to sob again. 'But that doesn't mean to say it's impossible.'

'What can we do?' Amy asked.

'Well, we can circulate their description and ask other officers to keep a look out,' said the policewoman. 'I suggest you put up notices on horsey websites that they have been stolen and make some reward posters to put up around the area. It always helps to keep an eye out at horse sales and fairs as well.'

Miss Mildew cleared her throat. They all turned to look at her. Sam's heart sank even further as she looked at Miss Mildew's sharp, thin face and her black hair scraped back into a severe bun. She didn't seem the type of person to offer words of comfort.

'You can try and get them back but it

is probably for the best if you do not get your hopes up,' she said. Janey sobbed even harder while Mum grabbed the table edge so hard her knuckles turned white. Her eyes were dark and shadowed and her brow was creased with pain. 'Horse thieves tend to get the animals they have taken out of the area as fast as they can. They will be on the other side of the country by the end of the week, where people won't be seeing your posters.' She gave a short, dry sigh and took another sip of tea.

It seemed that was too much for Mum

to take. She burst into tears and buried her face in her hands, while a weeping Janey tried to console her with an arm around the shoulders. Both the police officers looked at Miss Mildew with annoyance. She seemed oblivious to the upset her words had caused as she gazed at Mum and Janey and drank her tea.

Sam couldn't stand being in that room a second longer. She sidled towards the door as she heard one of the police officers try to persuade Mum and Janey that there was always hope. Amy got up and slipped out of the door behind her. The two sisters walked hand in hand through the yard, heads down, long blonde hair swinging around their faces as they tried to ignore the sad glances from other people. They didn't stop walking until they got to

Mulberry's stable, one of only eight on the bottom yard—a quiet, shady part of Meadow Vale Riding School.

They hid themselves inside and turned to look at each other. Sam wondered if she looked just like Amy did right now—white-faced, green eyes strained, and hair a mess.

'We're never going to see them again, are we?' she asked her big sister.

'Probably not,' Amy said, tears welling up in her eyes and chasing themselves

14

down her cheeks. Sam burst into tears and threw herself at her sister. They slid to the floor and sat there, their arms locked tight around each other as they sobbed.

'I can't . . . believe . . . we'll never see Velvet again,' hiccupped Amy. 'She's always been there.'

Mum had bought Velvet before Sam was born—Sam's earliest memory was of tipping her head back as far as it would go and that big black glossy horse filling her vision to every horizon. She remembered that huge head dropping down and the soft nose nuzzling her cheek, while the sweet scent of hay from Velvet's breath had washed over Sam's face. The first time Mum had put her on Velvet's back she felt as if she ruled the world, she was so high up. The rich warm smell of the big black mare had clung to her mother so that when Sam was little, they seemed like the same person. When Velvet wrapped her long neck around Sam and cuddled her close to her broad chest, it was as good as a hug from Mum.

Sam had watched while Mum had groomed Velvet, murmuring words of love that the big mare had answered with soft rumbles in her throat. She had envied them a little, how much they loved each other, and it was wonderful to feel that same love when she had bonded with Mulberry. Just like Mum with Velvet, Sam would brush Mulberry's black coat until it shone like a mirror while saying, 'I will love you, I will care for you, I will keep you forever,' and Mulberry had rumbled, just like Velvet, and pressed her nose against Sam's lips for a kiss. Sam's heart had swelled so much she thought it would burst.

The sisters sat and cried until they were exhausted and felt hollowed out. Amy went to look for Mum while Sam picked up a rake and made a feeble attempt to clean up Mulberry's stable. As she was working, a grey head looked around the door. It was Minnie the Moocher, the oldest animal on the yard. The little Shetland was one of the first ponies ever to work at Meadow Vale and now, in her retirement, she pleased herself by wandering around the yard.

'I heard what happened, young 'un,' Minnie said. 'I am sorry.'

'You didn't hear or see anything, did you, Minnie?' Sam asked hopefully. 'Anything at all that could tell us where they have been taken?'

The grizzled little mare shook her head. "Fraid not. I was out like a light all night, and, to be honest, my hearing isn't so good these days.'

'Oh,' Sam said, in a tiny voice. 'Well, if you think of anything . . . '

Minnie walked into the stable and nuzzled Sam's leg.

'I know you are feeling bad, but look at it this way,' Minnie said. 'You two-legs, you have big hearts. Some other little girl will love Mulberry just as much as you and you'll find another pony. Mulberry will be all right—Velvet and Lucy too. You'll all forget.'

Sam clenched her hands into fists. 'I won't forget Mulberry, not ever, and I won't stop looking for her,' she said, tears threatening to spill from her eyes again. 'We're bonded—she's the other half of me, like Velvet is to Mum and Lucy is to Janey. We can't just replace each other!'

Minnie sighed. 'I thought you might

say that. But there's a lot of heartbreak in thinking that way, little 'un, and lots of nice ponies that want loving homes.' She looked around the stable. 'Mulberry didn't leave any food behind, did she?'

Sam glared at her and Minnie had the decency to look embarrassed. She coughed. 'Just thought I would ask,' she said. 'Waste not, want not. You mind yourself now.'

The elderly Shetland shuffled off as Sam swept and tidied. The stable was already beginning to feel cold and deserted without Mulberry. Sam thought about what Minnie had said—about her trying to bond with another pony and Mulberry with another little girl. It made her heart hurt. She made herself a promise. There could never be another pony like Mulberry, not for her. She was never going to ride again.

Chapter 3

Mum drove them home in silence, her eyes red and swollen. Once indoors, Mum, Sam, and Amy each went to their rooms and curled up on their beds, their faces to the wall. They were like wounded animals—they couldn't even speak to each other.

Poor Dad didn't know what to do. He tried to talk to them, tried to cheer them up. He made cups of tea for Mum that she couldn't drink, and endless rounds of toast for Sam and Amy that stuck in their throats.

He pulled Sam's duvet over her, kissed her, and told her to try and get some sleep.

Sam was so exhausted from crying that she did sleep for a little while. She woke up thirsty and wandered downstairs to the kitchen for a drink of water. She stopped in the doorway to the living room and watched as Dad packed away all the photos of Velvet and Mulberry.

'What are you doing?' she asked.

Dad looked round and his face flushed red. 'I thought it might be easier on everyone if I just put these away for a little while,' he said, his big hands fluttering over the pile of photo frames. He looked down at his flitting hands and frowned, before shoving them firmly in his pockets.

'We don't know if they are gone for good yet,' Sam said.

'No, we don't,' Dad agreed, with forced cheerfulness, slapping a grin on his face. 'There's still hope yet. You've got to keep thinking positive.'

'I'm trying,' Sam said.

'That's my girl,' Dad said, still grinning away.

Sam frowned and then turned away to go to the kitchen. She could have sworn she heard Dad sigh with relief behind her. She took the glass back up to the room, sat on her bed, and looked around at all the posters and pictures she had stuck to the wall, of Mulberry and other ponies. She loved her busy, cluttered room with its pony pictures, pony duvet, and pony toys everywhere. But Dad was right—it did hurt her to look at all the pictures and be reminded of what she had lost.

But she wasn't going to take them down. If she did that, it would be like saying she had given up ever finding Mulberry, and she was never going to do that.

Sam listened for a moment to the unusually quiet house. There was no TV on, no sound of Mum getting dinner ready with the clatter of pots and the clink of cutlery, no beat of music coming from Amy's room. She was sure her father was trying very hard not to make the slightest noise. She snuggled back under her duvet, still in her riding clothes, and sighed. Her eyes were red and sore and she closed them for a moment to ease their stinging. Her clothes were old ones that she had worn yesterday and she pulled a sleeve down over her hand and held it to her nose. She breathed deeply and was surrounded by

the rich, tangy smell of Mulberry. Fresh tears welled slowly beneath her lids and kissed her eyes cool.

Sam didn't know how she fell asleep but she must have drifted off. Dreams came tumbling out of her imagination, fragments and glimpses of nonsense that ran into each other without pause, like a film made of clips from lots of other movies. But she had one dream that felt very real. She was sitting on a high garden wall bordering a little country lane. There was a cornflower-blue sky above her and sunshine on her face and Mulberry, walking up and down the lane, passing just centimetres from Sam's feet. In her dream, Sam leaned down and stretched her fingers out, and each time Mulberry walked past her, she could just about brush Mulberry's glossy black coat and wiry mane with the tips of her fingers. She couldn't get any closer and Mulberry didn't speak to her as she marched up and down.

The ringing of the telephone woke Sam up and she found her hand clenched into a tight fist. She almost expected to see some of the long black hairs from Mulberry's mane as she uncurled her fingers, the dream had felt that real. She sat up in bed—it was dark outside and the colours of her room had faded to black and white in the rays of moonlight that poured in through her thin curtains. She felt as though her head had been stuffed with cotton wool and she was so thirsty her tongue stuck to the roof of her mouth. She rubbed a hand over her hair and wondered who was calling.

Sam squealed in fright as the door to her room burst open and bounced off the wall behind it. Dad switched on the light, making Sam squint, and he was grinning from ear to ear again, only this time the smile didn't look forced.

'She's back, Sam!' he said. 'Mulberry has been found!'

Chapter 4

Sam could hardly breathe as Mum drove as fast as she could to the yard. Dad and Amy had come with them too and Sam felt she could cut the tension in the car with a knife. They had all been so excited when Dad had told them the news, all trying to speak at once, but, now they were on their way to the yard, all of them were thinking the same thing.

What if the pony who had come back wasn't Mulberry? Was it possible someone had made a mistake?

All the lights were on in the yard as they drove up, the whole place shining brilliantly in the blue velvety dark of the countryside. The horses looked grumpy and tired with all the noise and the fuss as Miss Mildew, her long hair in a loose braid hanging over one shoulder and a jumper and wellies pulled over her pyjamas, waited for them in the car park.

Sam had her seat belt off and was opening the door before Mum had switched the engine off.

'Is it her? Is it really her?' she asked Miss Mildew, breathless with excitement.

'Honestly, Miss Grey, I think I would be able to recognize Mulberry,' said Miss Mildew, raising one thin black eyebrow. 'Do you really think I would have dragged your parents out of bed if I wasn't sure?'

Sam ignored the acid sarcasm in Miss Mildew's voice and raced to the bottom yard and Mulberry's stable. Even as she ran towards it, she could tell it felt different. It felt warmer. She looked over the door and there was beautiful, black, glossy Mulberry, munching on a hay net as if she had just been brought in from the field.

'MULBERRY!' screeched Sam, sliding

31

the door bolts back and hurling herself at the stocky little mare. She heard the mare say, 'Oof, watch it, you're getting bigger, you know!' as she wrapped her arms around Mulberry's long neck and buried her face in her thick, bushy mane. Mulberry looked as if she had been dragged through a hedge backwards. Her coat was dusty, she had scratches on her soft nose, and her mane had bits of twigs and leaves caught in it.

'You came back to me!' Sam said, her face nearly splitting from her big smile. 'I knew you would if you could!'

'Funnily enough, it seems that is exactly what she did,' Miss Mildew said. Sam looked up to see Miss Mildew, Dad, Mum, and Amy looking in at herself and Mulberry. 'I know the way children love to exaggerate, especially when it comes to their pets, but Mulberry found her way back here all by herself.'

'You mean, nobody found her?' Mum asked, the hope fading a little in her face.

'No, Mulberry walked back onto the yard all by herself about an hour ago,' Miss Mildew said. 'I have no idea where she came from.'

'So no one knows where Velvet and Lucy are?' Mum asked, her face sagging with sadness again.

'I'm afraid not,' Miss Mildew said. 'But if Mulberry managed to escape and wander off, perhaps the other two did as well. I have called the local yards and given them Velvet and Lucy's descriptions and asked them to keep an eye out.'

Dad put an arm around Mum's shoulder. 'It's like I said, love, there is always hope,' he said. 'We've got one back—only two more to go.'

Mum said nothing but she put her hand over the stable door and stroked Mulberry's soft nose. The little mare rumbled in her throat and nuzzled at Mum's fingers. 'At least we have you, little lady,' she whispered. Sam went still at the pain in her mother's face, while Mulberry gazed back at Mum with her dark eyes and licked at her fingers.

Dad cleared his throat. 'Why don't we leave these two to get to know each other again?' he said. 'Miss Mildew, I am sure we could all do with a cup of tea.'

'Well,' Miss Mildew said, 'it's rather late, but I don't suppose there is much chance I will get back to sleep tonight with all this fuss and excitement, so it wouldn't do any harm to make some.'

'That is very good of you,' Dad said as they all walked away, with just a hint of laughter in his voice.

Sam waited until she was sure they were all out of earshot and then kissed Mulberry on the cheek.

'Oh, Mulberry,' she said. 'Where have

you been? I can't believe I got you back!'
The little mare snorted and shook her
mane. "Course I came back—I could
hardly leave you on your own,
could I? Who knows what sort
of trouble you would get
yourself into without me
to take care of you?'

Sam giggled as
Mulberry pushed
against her cheek
with her nose and
gave her a big,
sloppy lick.

'I love you too,
Mulberry,' she said.
'Steady on—no need to go all mushy on
me,' Mulberry said. She cocked her head
to one side. 'You haven't been riding any

other ponies while I've been gone, have you?'

Sam squealed with laughter as the pony glared at her with an expression of fierce jealousy. She wrapped her arms around her neck again. 'Don't be daft! You've only been gone one day!'

'That's my girl!' Mulberry said, nuzzling Sam's neck. Then she went still and her head shot up in the air, ears pricked and nostrils flared to take in big snorts of air. 'Hang on. What's that smell?' Mulberry put her nose to the ground and sniffed all around like a dog. 'Minnie the Moocher's been in here, hasn't she?!'

'Only for a minute,' Sam said. 'She was telling me how sorry she was that you had been stolen.'

'Ha! A likely story,' Mulberry snorted.

'It's true!' Sam said.

Mulberry narrowed her eyes at Sam. 'So she didn't ask for any food, then? None at all?'

'Well, she did ask if you had left any food behind,' Sam said. 'She said she didn't want anything going to waste if it wasn't going to get eaten. Which is reasonable enough, when you think about it.'

'I knew it!' Mulberry said, stamping a little hoof and shaking her mane, which seemed to be getting stiffer with rage. 'She couldn't wait until the stable got cold, could she? Oh no, not that one! She'd have your hay net off its hook as soon as your back is turned.'

'Oh, Mulberry, don't worry about it,' Sam said. 'I promise, she didn't get a mouthful of any feed meant for you—not so much as a single piece of hay.' She reached up and rubbed the mare between the eyes. Mulberry sighed and lidded her eyes with contentment. 'You're back now and that's all that matters. I'm going to spoil you with lots of green apples and extra hay.'

Mulberry looked up, her black eyes bright. 'How about some hard feed?'

'Don't push your luck,' Sam said.

Mulberry yawned. 'You know what? I've been walking for ages and it's pretty late. I could do with a bit of sleep seeing as unlike you lazy two-legs I tend to wake up at the same time as the birds around here. Why don't you go home and get some sleep and get back here tomorrow, bright and early? We've got a lot to talk about.'

'Like where Velvet and Lucy are? We need to get them back, Mulberry—you saw the state Mum is in,' Sam said. 'Janey isn't much better. Do you know where they are?'

'That's for me to know and you to find out, isn't it?' Mulberry said, blinking slowly as her eyelids grew heavier and heavier with sleep. 'Toddle off to your own bed now and come back in a few hours for a chat. All will be revealed then.'

Chapter 5

Sam collapsed into bed as soon as she got home. She was so tired she slept right through her alarm and it was nearly eleven o'clock in the morning before she did wake up. The sun was riding high in the sky and the kitchen was getting hot as the sun beamed through the patio doors. Mum was sipping a drink at the table, her eyes rimmed with dark shadows. She looked pale and Sam felt guilty about asking her to give her a lift to the stables.

'Do you mind driving me up to Meadow Vale, Mum?' Sam asked, her cheeks flaming hot and her voice coming out

as just a whisper. 'I really wanted to see Mulberry, if that's OK with you?'

Mum smiled at her but her eyes stayed sad. 'Of course I don't mind, Sam. I am so glad you have your Mulberry back, really, I am.'

'We might have Velvet home soon.'

'Maybe, darling, maybe.'

But Mum didn't say anything in the car and when they got to Meadow Vale she kept her seat belt on and the engine running. 'I don't think I will stay today,' she said to Sam. 'I think I will go into town and do some shopping instead. Get Miss Mildew or Janey to give me a ring when you want picking up.'

Sam looked at her mother's sad eyes and swallowed, so her voice wouldn't come out squeaky. 'Sure,' she said. She shut the car door and waved goodbye as her mother drove out of the yard. She could see Janey putting a pony away in the barn and raised her hand to say hello, but Janey had sunglasses on and Sam didn't think she saw her. She stopped in the tack room and picked up some grooming brushes before walking over to Mulberry's stable.

Mulberry was awake and munching on another big hay net. Someone had mucked her out for Sam and laid down fresh shavings so the whole stable smelt sweet. Sam smiled—it was probably Janey.

'I brought some brushes,' she said to Mulberry, holding them up and waggling them. 'How about a good groom—get all that rubbish out of your mane?'

Mulberry wriggled her body with delight, almost like a puppy. 'Oooh, lovely. We can talk while you're doing it.'

Sam loved grooming Mulberry—she found the rhythm of running the brush over Mulberry's body soothing. Her arms and hands knew what to do without her thinking about it and she could let her mind drift while the brush rippled over Mulberry's neck and shoulders, flicked left and right over the whorl of hair between her hind legs and her rib cage, and smoothed out the fine hair over her thin-skinned belly. While they talked, Mulberry's coat began to gleam again as the brush polished her.

'How did you manage to get away, Mulberry?'

'Oh, it was hard!' Mulberry said, puffing up her chest. 'They locked me in a dark and dingy stable and I had to kick the door into splinters to get loose. The noise brought the thieves running and I had to battle my way through a crowd of about twenty men, all trying to catch me with ropes and head collars. Big, huge blokes they were but I knew I had to get back to you so I just put my head down . . . '

'They left the stable door open by

mistake, didn't they?' Sam said, putting her hands on her hips and looking sternly at Mulberry. The little black mare cocked her head to one side and snorted.

'They might have done,' she said. 'But that would make a very boring story.'

Sam laughed and kissed Mulberry on the nose. 'I don't care how you got away, Mulberry, as long as you are back. I'm just sorry that Velvet and Lucy couldn't get away as well.'

'That's what I wanted to talk to you about,' Mulberry said. 'I know where they are being kept.'

Sam stopped breathing, just for a second, as what Mulberry said sank into her sleep-deprived brain.

'Mulberry, that's fantastic!' she said, a smile lighting up her face. 'We can tell the police and we can get Velvet and Lucy back for Mum and Janey! What are the stables called?'

'I don't know,' Mulberry said, lifting a back leg and scratching herself behind an ear with a hoof.

'Well, what road is it on?'

'Dunno that either.'

The smile dropped from Sam's face and she could feel the fizzy feeling of hope dying down in her stomach. 'I thought you said you knew where it was?'

'I know where it is, but I don't know what anything is called,' Mulberry said. 'No one mentioned any names in front of me and I can't read. But I'd know how to find it again—it isn't that far.'

'Great!' Sam said. 'Give me the directions and I'll . . . '

'You'll what?' Mulberry said, looking hard at Sam. 'Give directions and a description of the place to your parents, the police? When they ask you how you know for sure this is where Velvet and Lucy are being kept, what are you going to say—your pony told you?'

'Oh . . . ' Sam said.

'Exactly,' Mulberry said. 'No one is going to believe you, Sam.'

'But we can't just leave them there!' Sam said.

'No, we can't,' Mulberry agreed.

Sam had been expecting an argument from Mulberry and had been drawing breath to yell over her. She was so surprised Mulberry was agreeing with her without putting up the slightest fight that she almost choked on that indrawn breath.

'I thought you didn't like Velvet or Lucy?' she asked.

'I don't,' Mulberry said. 'Velvet is a bossyboots while Lucy has a right gob on her. But you haven't seen that yard.' Mulberry shuddered. 'It's dirty and broken, with rubbish strewn about and rats running around everywhere. Those men that took us were rough with their hands and I saw them beat Velvet with a whip when she wouldn't get off the lorry for them.' Mulberry shook her head sadly. 'She was trying hard to get back to your mum. Lucy turned her face against the wall of the stable they put her in when she realized she couldn't get away. Who knows where they will end up if we don't get them out—them and the others.'

'What others?' Sam asked. 'There are more?'

'Oh, yes,' Mulberry said. 'Those thieves have been busy. There is another pony on that yard as well and even a foal that really isn't old enough to be away from its mother. I could hear the poor little thing crying.' Mulberry shook her head. 'What kind of person takes a foal away from its mother?'

'What are you going to do?'

Mulberry looked at Sam again. 'We are going back there tonight and we are going to break them all out.'

'Me?' Sam squeaked in terror.

'Unless I grow thumbs in the next couple of hours I'm not going to be able to undo bolts, am I? And again, I ask the same question—which is getting tedious, by the way—HOW are you going to tell anyone else about this? We haven't got much time either. We've got to go tonight because they are moving them all on tomorrow—I heard them say so.'

'What happens if we get caught?' Sam said. 'How are we supposed to get all those animals away from twenty men?!'

Mulberry looked embarrassed. 'I may have exaggerated that story a little, you know, for dramatic impact.'

'That's a shocker,' Sam said. 'So how many thieves are there, really?'

'Um, two,' Mulberry said. 'That improves our chances, eh?'

'That's still two grown-ups,' Sam pointed out.

'You'll have me with you,' Mulberry said. 'That's as good as bringing your own army.'

Sam thought for a second. 'How am I supposed to get out of the house? How am I supposed to get here? Mum normally drives me—it could take an hour to walk here on my own and someone might see me and bring me straight home.'

'You have to think of something, Sam,' Mulberry said. 'We only have tonight to get them back and I can't do this on my own.'

Sam frowned and waited for a light-bulb moment. After a few minutes, it was like someone had flicked the 'on' switch in her brain.

'I think I might know a way,' she said.

Chapter 6

Meadow Vale ran a pony camp every summer that all the students looked forward to. The older ones, like Amy, often stayed overnight in a mobile home that was parked at the back of Miss Mildew's house, so they could be within earshot. The best chance Sam had of sneaking off with Mulberry tonight depended on her not leaving the yard at all.

Sam hated talking to Miss Mildew. She never smiled and she always made Sam feel nervous. Sam's stomach flip-flopped, her legs went rubbery, and she never knew what to do with her hands when she had to talk to her. But she had to do this. So she took a deep breath and knocked on Miss Mildew's office door.

'Come in,' said Miss Mildew, sharply. Sam swallowed and opened the door.

Miss Mildew was sorting through some papers on her desk. She barely looked up as Sam walked over. 'What can I do for you, Miss Grey?'

Sam cleared her throat. 'I wanted to stay overnight in the mobile home tonight, if that is OK with you?'

Miss Mildew looked at Sam and raised an eyebrow. 'Why on earth would you want to do that?'

'I just . . . I just want to stay close to Mulberry tonight,' Sam said.

Miss Mildew frowned. 'It is highly unlikely that the thieves are going to return just for Mulberry. She is perfectly safe, Miss Grey.'

'Oh, I know,' Sam said. 'But still, I'd like to stay tonight, if it's all right with you?'

Miss Mildew thought about this for a second and then sighed. 'Let me speak to your mother first, Miss Grey. Then I shall decide what is "all right".'

Sam nodded, her insides turning to ice. Miss Mildew didn't sound as though she was in the mood to say 'yes'. She went outside and closed the door but, instead of sitting in a hard plastic chair Miss Mildew had for waiting students, Sam pressed her ear to the door.

It was hard to hear what Miss Mildew was saying as she was keeping her voice low, almost as if she knew Sam was eavesdropping. Sam could only hear the odd word, such as 'traumatic' and 'reassurance'. She had no idea if Miss Mildew was going to let her stay or not.

The murmuring stopped and Sam had just enough time to scoot over to the chair before Miss Mildew opened the door. 'Your mother is on her way up, Miss Grey. We will wait for her to arrive and then I will make a decision.'

Sam nodded and whispered a 'thank
you' at Miss Mildew's unsmiling face
before escaping through the yard back to
Mulberry's stable. Mulberry popped her
head over her stable door as soon as she
heard Sam's footsteps and gave an excited
whinny.

'Did it work?' she asked.

'I don't know,' Sam said miserably. 'I don't think it did. Mum is on her way up and Miss Mildew was using some funny words when she was talking to her on the phone.'

Mulberry flattened her ears and her face went tight with worry. 'You have to come with me,' she said. 'I won't be able to get Velvet and Lucy and the others free without you.'

'I know,' Sam said. She opened the door and sat on the floor of Mulberry's stable. The little mare dropped her head down and nuzzled Sam's cheek with her nose. Sam wrapped her arms around Mulberry's neck and snuggled close. Her stomach was tying itself up in knots, she was so worried.

It felt as though it took hours for Mum to arrive. Sam was still sitting in Mulberry's stable when she heard footsteps echoing across the yard. She peeped over the door to see Mum and Miss Mildew walking towards the stable. Mum was smiling and she had a bag in her hand. Sam's tummy unknotted, just a tiny bit.

'Come here and give me a hug,' Mum said, holding out her other hand. Sam slipped out of the stable and cuddled close to her mother's side, breathing in

the chocolatey smell of her skin cream. Mum stroked Sam's hair.

'Miss Mildew tells me you want to stay here tonight, to be close to Mulberry. Is that right?' Mum asked.

Sam nodded.

'I know it was frightening when Mulberry was gone but she's back now and those bad men won't be coming back for her,' Mum said. 'You're not going to lose her again.'

'I know,' Sam said. 'But I can't help worrying.' As she said it, she realized it was true. The thought of letting Mulberry out of her sight made her chest feel tight and sore.

Mum smiled. 'I know that feeling,' she said. 'Miss Mildew has kindly agreed to let you stay tonight but you will sleep in the spare bedroom in her house. You're far too young to be in the mobile home on your own.'

'It will be just for tonight though, Miss Grey,' Miss Mildew said. 'I know you have had a shock but we all have to start getting back to normal sooner or later.'

The smile wavered on Mum's face just a little. Sam realized that unless she got Velvet back, things would never ever be normal for Mum again. 'Thank you very much, Miss Mildew,' she said.

Miss Mildew's mouth twitched and she patted Sam's head like she was a puppy. 'Let me show you your room.'

Sam couldn't believe that she was following Miss Mildew into the Forbidden Place, the one part of the yard no one ever went or dared disturb Miss Mildew—the bungalow she lived in, surrounded by a little garden, behind the stables.

It was cool and dark in the bungalow. Everything was very neat and clean—it didn't actually look as though anyone lived there at all. There were no magazines or papers lying around, no spare shoes, no dirty teacups like there were at Sam's house. Miss Mildew led the way down a shadowy hallway and opened the door to a single room. It smelt of air freshener and the single bed was made up so neatly and tightly, it looked as if Sam could bounce a coin off it. She was relieved to see the window was a sash—so she had plenty of room to squeeze through—and that the room faced the back of Mulberry's stable.

'I brought you a change of clothes and some pyjamas,' Mum said, putting the bag on the bed. 'Your toothbrush is in there as well. Do you fancy getting some dinner, just you and me?'

So that was how Sam got Mum all to herself that evening, sharing a pizza at a local restaurant with her and talking like mad to fill the silence. Mum was heartbroken but Sam knew she was trying so hard to make her feel better about Mulberry being back. Now and then, her parents gave Sam a glimpse of how much they loved her. Sam wished she could tell her mother everything, wished she could put her arms around her and say everything would be OK, that Velvet would be home soon. But she knew Mulberry was right— no one would believe her if she told the truth. She thought about Janey and the way the sunglasses had covered half her face. Janey had probably been crying all night as well. Any nerves Sam felt about tonight were disappearing as she realized how much two people she really loved were suffering. And what must Velvet and Lucy be feeling, all alone, with strangers?

Mum drove her back to the yard and she went into the sitting room to say goodnight to Miss Mildew. The yard owner was reading her book, her back ramrod straight, even when she was supposed to be relaxing.

'Goodness me, Miss Grey, is that the time?' she said, looking at the clock. 'Off to bed for both of us. Horses like their breakfast at dawn so it's an early start.'

Sam tackled the bed. The sheets and blankets were tucked around the mattress so tightly, it was a real effort to pull them back enough for her to get into the bed. She had to force her feet and legs underneath them and, as she pulled them up to her chin to hide the fact she was still in her T-shirt and jodhpurs, she felt as if she were being pressed between the pages of a book. She lay there, as stiff as a mummy, and waited for Miss Mildew to go to bed and for the bungalow to go quiet.

As soon as Sam thought the coast was clear, she half slid, half fell out of the bed, pulled on her riding boots, and crept over to the window. It was a clear night and the moonlight poured through the window like liquid silver. She gently pushed back the window lock and slowly, very slowly, lifted the sash window. It slid up smoothly, with only a slight rustle of wood scraping against wood and she swung her legs over the sill, dropped to the garden below, and ran for Mulberry's stable.

Chapter 7

'About time—I thought you had fallen asleep!' Mulberry hissed in what sounded to Sam like a very loud whisper. She winced and put her finger to her lips.

'That's a laugh,' Mulberry said. 'Do you have any idea how loud you two-legs are when you move about? I could hear you opening the window!'

Sam sighed. 'I know how much you love to argue, Mulberry . . . ' she said.

'I don't argue, I merely have heated discussions,' Mulberry interrupted. 'Saying I argue all the time makes me sound so bad-tempered.'

Sam really had to bite her tongue to avoid saying something that would have them arguing all night. Mulberry's humongous ego didn't give Mulberry a rose-tinted view of herself, it made her blind as a bat to her faults.

'I'm here now,' Sam whispered, sliding back the bolt on the top of Mulberry's door and flipping the kick bolt at the bottom back with her foot. 'So let's get you tacked up and go.'

'How do you reckon you are going to do that, genius?' Mulberry asked. 'The tack room is locked.'

Sam groaned. She forgot Miss Mildew would have locked the tack room up tight before going to bed. All the saddles and the bridles on the yard were far too valuable to be left in an unlocked room.

'What are we going to do?' she asked Mulberry.

'Simple—you're just going to have to ride me bareback and hold onto my mane,' Mulberry shrugged.

'I can't—I've never ridden bareback before!' Sam said.

'Well, right about now is a fantastic time to start learning,' Mulberry said as she pushed the door open and stepped out onto the yard. 'Let's get out of here first. Quiet as you can—we don't want to wake up a goody two-shoes who will neigh its head off and let everyone know what we are up to.'

So the two of them tiptoed as quietly as they could through the sleeping yard. Sam looked nervously at the stables full of slumbering horses and ponies, waiting for one of them to wake up.

As they passed the barn she looked in on the Shetlands. If anyone was going to wake up and cause a racket it would be Apricot, Mickey, and Turbo. But each of them was lying flat out on their straw bed, their little pot bellies rising and falling slowly as they dreamed. In the cob part of the barn, cautious, sensible Basil was sleeping standing up, his nose touching his broad chest and deep snores rumbling down his

long face and through his big nostrils. Sam looked again at the Shetlands—she could have sworn she saw the gleam of an open eye, but none of them moved. It must have been a trick of the light. Mulberry nuzzled her impatiently and the two of them walked past the office and turned onto the driveway.

They were almost at the gate when they heard the clang of metal and the trip trap of little hooves. They both froze. 'Did you hear that?' Sam whispered.

'Keep going,' Mulberry said through clenched teeth. 'Do NOT look behind. You'll only encourage them.'

Someone coughed behind Sam. The cough was coming from somewhere by her knees. She couldn't help herself—she turned around and looked down.

Apricot was staring up at her with an expression of mock innocence, her shaggy blonde forelock hanging in her big brown eyes. 'Whatcha doin'?' she asked.

'Nothing!' Mulberry snapped, before Sam could say anything. 'Go back to the barn and mind your own business.' Sam heard another clang and saw Turbo struggling to squeeze under the gate to the barn, his fat belly squishing against the ground.

'It don't look like nothing,' Apricot said,

her eyes never leaving Sam's. 'Does it look like nothing to you, Mickey?'

'No, Apricot, it does not,' Mickey said. 'It looks as if our dear friend, Mulberry, is sneaking off the yard without permission.'

'That's naughty,' Apricot said. 'Do you think the two-legs has permission from her mum to go sneaking off with Mulberry?'

'Probably not, seeing as they are being so sneaky,' Mickey said.

'That's very naughty,' Apricot said.

'Very, very naughty,' Mickey agreed. 'I'm shocked, I really am.'

'Do you think we should raise the alarm?' Apricot asked. 'I don't think I would sleep easy tonight, knowing this little two-legs was out and about without her mummy's permission. That would give me bad dreams, it would.'

'Please, don't do that!' Sam pleaded.

'Give me one good reason why I shouldn't,' Apricot said.

'Don't say a word, Sam!' Mulberry hissed.

'Mulberry knows where Velvet and Lucy are being kept by the thieves. They have other ponies and a little foal too,' Sam said. 'We're going to get them back.'

'Are you now?' Apricot said. She and Mickey pricked up their ears and their dark eyes gleamed with excitement.

'I'm wasting my breath talking to you,' Mulberry said to Sam. 'They will want to come now.'

'Too right we do,' Mickey said. 'Why should you have all the fun?'

'It's hardly going to be fun!' Sam protested.

'Is there a chance of getting to kick someone?' Apricot asked.

'Probably, if it all goes wrong,' Mulberry said. 'Maybe even bite someone as well. Two-legs don't like thieves—no one is going to object if we are forced to rough 'em up a bit, in self-defence, of course.'

'Mickey's right, that sounds like fun,' Apricot said. 'Count us in.'

Mulberry narrowed her eyes at Apricot. 'Who said you're coming?'

Apricot narrowed her eyes back and pawed the ground in temper. 'I did.'

'We're not messing around here,' Mulberry said. 'We've only got one night to rescue Velvet, Lucy, and the others.'

'If things get out of hand, you're going to need us,' Mickey said.

'We've got skills,' Apricot said. They all

looked at Turbo who had managed to get most of his belly out from under the gate. His face was scrunched up with pain and he was panting with the effort as he finally pulled his pot belly free with a pop and a clang as the gate to the barn bounced on its hinges.

'Hidden skills,' Apricot said, as Turbo trotted over.

'You're not coming,' Mulberry said.

'Fine,' Mickey said. 'Then we're just going to run around the yard, neighing very loudly, and get everyone up.'

'Mildew might be so hard of hearing that she doesn't notice a couple of horses getting nicked quietly in the middle of the night but not even she can sleep through the whole yard neighing,' Apricot said.

Mulberry narrowed her eyes even further so they were just tiny slits of black rage. Apricot glared back and Sam fidgeted nervously as the two ponies tried to outstare each other.

'Fine,' spat Mulberry. 'You can come, just keep quiet.'

'Where are we going?' Turbo asked.

'We're going on a top-secret mission, Tub Tubs, where we could get into a lot of trouble and may have to kick and bite people,' Apricot said.

'Awesome!' Turbo said and cantered out of the yard and up the road, without asking anyone what they were doing or even which direction they should be going in.

'Give me strength,' Mulberry sighed.

Chapter 8

'We need to stay off the road,' Mulberry said. 'We don't want anyone to spot us.'

Apricot snorted. 'Who's up at this time of night?'

'Two-legs run around all night,' Mulberry said. 'They are too lazy to start the day at dawn like animals do. Here, Sam, hop up on my back—it will be slow going if you are on foot.'

'I'm scared I'm going to fall off,' Sam said.

'Don't be daft,' Mulberry said. When have I ever dropped you?' Sam raised an eyebrow.

'By mistake,' added Mulberry quickly.

'I don't know . . . '

'Sam, if you want a happy ending to tonight, you're going to have to risk a few broken bones,' Mulberry said.

'Well, that just fills me with confidence!' Sam said.

Apricot butted her in the side with her head. 'Stop being a ninny and get on. You're wasting time!'

Sam took a deep breath and scrambled awkwardly onto Mulberry's broad, short back. The mare winced as Sam dragged herself upright by hanging onto Mulberry's thick, long mane.

'Ouch!' Mulberry said, looking around at Sam and pulling a face. 'And you were worried you were the one who was going to get hurt?!'

Sam blushed. 'Sorry,' she said.

'Never mind,' Mulberry said. 'But we are going to have to practise this a bit more at home. You never know when bareback riding is going to come in handy. Hold on tight!'

Sam tried not to scream as the ponies all set off at a jog. She felt very insecure without a saddle to hold her in place, stirrups to brace herself against, and reins to hold on to. She cringed at the feel of Mulberry's spine digging into her bottom but it didn't seem to hurt the mare. It felt weird to feel every ripple of muscle against her legs as Mulberry moved. To make it worse, the ponies were going across the surrounding fields, scrabbling through hedgerows and trotting along rutted earth tracks which had had been dried and baked by the summer

sun to iron hardness. The tough little blue
hooves of the native ponies skipped over
everything. Not once did Mulberry or any
of the Shetlands stumble. Their round,
short bodies and neat little feet were built
for rough going—Mulberry wasn't going
to drop Sam. Even so, it took all of her will
power not to look down at the ground as

she let her legs dangle around Mulberry's sides. The little mare's summer coat was as smooth and slippery as satin and the only thing keeping Sam on her back was balance. Jancy had always warned her to look where she was going—her head was the heaviest part of her body. 'Always look where you are going if you want to stay balanced,' Janey had said, over and over again in her riding lessons. 'And if you keep looking at the ground, guess where you will end up?' So Sam looked straight ahead and tried to relax as much as possible. If her body tensed up, that could make her fall off as well!

It didn't help when Mulberry looked over her shoulder at her and said, 'You can breathe, you know.'

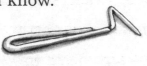

It didn't take long for the countryside around them to become unfamiliar, turned to black and white by the light of the summer moon that hung heavy and ripe in the sky. Sam was utterly lost and she worried that Mulberry was as well.

'Are you sure you know where you are going,' she asked.

Mulberry snorted. 'Course I do!'

'But you can't read and you've only been there once,' Sam said.

'Doesn't matter,' Mulberry said. 'I've got an animal's sense of direction. I only have to be somewhere once and I know where I am going. Ever wondered how dogs and cats make their way across the country to their old home when their owners move? It's like an extra sense that we've got.'

'Turbo gets lost every time he escapes from the barn,' Apricot said.

'I do not!' Turbo protested, his little legs blurring as he trotted fast to keep up with Mulberry.

'Do too!' Mickey said.

'Well, maybe I do the odd time but I always turn myself in at the police station,' Turbo said cheerfully. 'I know where that is.'

The countryside was still and quiet as they trotted on. Sam shivered a little in

the cool night
air and dug her
hands deep into
Mulberry's thick black
mane. There were no street-
lights out here and no lights
on in any of the houses they
came across. Fields empty of
livestock stretched around
them—they could have
been on the surface of
the moon, it was so
deserted. Far from
being the terrify-
ing experience
Sam had
expected,

she found herself fighting against sleep. The only scary moment they had was when some security lights suddenly came on as they skirted around the back of a farmhouse, illuminating the building in a blaze of light. A dog started barking, a very big dog from the sound of it, and they all flattened themselves against the ground to avoid detection, Sam rolling from Mulberry's back and hiding behind her body. Well, the Shetlands tried to flatten themselves but they really just squished their bellies against the ground like half-inflated beach balls. They all held their breath as they heard a door bang and a man's voice shouting at the dog to be quiet. The dog went into a frenzy of barking and Sam worried that its owner might decide to have a look around and see what had upset it. But after a few moments, the dog's barks subsided and the man went back inside. Everything turned to silver again as the security light blinked off but Mulberry hissed a warning at them when they went to get up.

'Stay still a moment,' she said. 'I want to make sure that stupid dog has gone back to sleep.'

So they crouched in the long grass behind the farmhouse while Mulberry flicked her ears towards it, straining to pick up on any sound. Mulberry was as still as a statue, just a darker patch

of black in the night, but the Shetlands
started to fidget.

'Is it me, or is it cold tonight?'
Turbo asked.

'It's you,' Apricot said. 'It's the height of
summer, you wally-brain.'

'Well, I'm bloomin' freezing,' Turbo
said.

'If you can feel your toes, you're OK,'
Mickey said.

A look of panic washed over Turbo's face. 'I can't feel them . . . oh, hang on.' Apricot and Mickey's shoulders shook as they tried to stifle their giggles. Turbo looked at them reproachfully. 'That's just mean.'

'I can't believe you fell for that,' Apricot said, snot flying out her nose as she snorted.

'Can't you lot shut up?' Mulberry growled.

'Oh, relax!' Apricot whispered, standing up and giving a little shake. 'Fido has obviously gone back to sleep. Let's get moving because this whole outing is getting a bit boring. If things don't liven up soon, I'm going home to my nice warm bed.'

'I didn't ask you to come along,' Mulberry said as Sam climbed onto her back.

'Like that would have made any difference,' Apricot said as the Shetlands trotted off.

'I hate that mouthy little mare, I really do,' Mulberry said to Sam. 'I told you not to make eye contact with her—you only encourage them when you give them attention.'

'They might be useful though, Mulberry,'
Sam said. 'Apricot does enjoy fighting for
the sake of it.'

'I never thought I would hear myself say
this, but we don't want a fight, young 'un,'
Mulberry said. 'The plan is that you slide
the bolts back on all those stable doors and
we slip out of there while those thieves
are fast asleep, as quick and quiet as we
slipped in.'

Sam swallowed. 'What's plan B if it all
goes wrong?'

'We set the ninja Shetlands on them
and we make a run for it,' Mulberry said
grimly.

Chapter 9

Sam was losing all track of time. She couldn't make out what her watch read in the dark and she could only pray they were not too far from home. Whatever happened tonight, they had to be back before dawn, otherwise Miss Mildew would find Sam's bed empty in the morning. After what felt like an eternity, Mulberry led them around the back of a stable yard.

'We're here,' Mulberry said, as Sam slid to the ground, her knees almost buckling as her legs cramped. The Shetlands sniffed at the air, their faces sour with disapproval.

'It doesn't smell like they muck out much,' Mickey said.

'Or keep their hay nice and dry,' Apricot said. 'I'm definitely getting a whiff of mouldy hay. Yuck!'

Mulberry nuzzled at Sam and blew her warm breath gently into her face as Sam shivered next to her with fright, one arm draped around Mulberry's neck to keep herself upright.

'Duck under that fence, young 'un, and slip back those bolts,' she said. 'As soon as you get the last door open, come back here and we'll go round waking them all up and getting them to walk out. That foal might need a bit of persuading—poor little thing was terrified.'

'I know how it feels,' Sam said, trying to stop her teeth from chattering.

'Don't you worry,' Mulberry said. 'I can see the whole yard from here, clear as day with this moon. If those thieves wake up and come out, I'll be onto them before they can get anywhere near you.'

'What if they can move faster than you?' Sam asked.

'Nothing and no one can move faster than me when you're in trouble,' Mulberry said fiercely.

'And we'll be right behind her,' Apricot said.

Sam smiled weakly and kissed Mulberry on the nose. 'Wish me luck,' she said.

'You've got me, you don't need luck,' Mulberry said. 'I want you back here in five minutes—we'll do the rest.'

So Sam took a deep breath and crawled under the fence. She crept slowly towards

the stable block, trying to stare at the dark and silent house and catch a glimpse of Velvet and Lucy at the same time.

The yard was not only dirty, it was messy as well. Sam had to be careful where she put her feet as the ground was littered with discarded feed buckets, a rake, lead ropes, and grooming brushes. She finally reached the first stable and crouched down to make herself as small as possible. She reached up to the iron bolt, her blood pounding in her ears. Her breathing seeming to roar in the night. She tried to make it as quiet as possible, sucking in small, shallow breaths, but she was sure the lack of oxygen was getting to her. Sweat dripped off her forehead. *Just slip the bolt back and move on to the next one,* she thought to herself. *This will all be over in minutes and we can all go home.*

Her stomach turned to ice and she forgot to breathe altogether as her searching fingers closed around something she hadn't been expecting. There was a padlock on the stable door! She stood up quickly and tugged on it, hoping that it might not be locked. But the padlock didn't budge— it was locked up tight. Sam looked down the row of stable doors and her heart sank as she saw what she had missed as she had tried to make her way unseen across the yard. Every single door was padlocked. The thieves must have decided not to take any chances after Mulberry had made her escape. Nothing was getting in or out of those stables without a key.

A big, dark head loomed out from the gloom of the stable and a familiar scent washed over Sam. 'Velvet!' she whispered, putting her hand up to stroke the big mare's cheek.

'Sam!' Velvet said in amazement. 'What on earth are you doing here?'

'We came to get you,' Sam said. 'But the doors are locked.'

'Who is "we"?' Velvet asked.

'Mulberry and the Shetlands,' Sam said. 'Mulberry knew where they were keeping you . . . '

'Mulberry—I should have known!' Velvet said. 'I don't expect anything else from those nutcase Shetlands but Mulberry really should know better than to put you in harm's way!'

'She wanted to save you and Lucy—

we both did,' Sam said. 'Mum and Janey can't stop crying—we have to get you home.'

Velvet laid her ears back against her head, her eyes filled with despair. 'I miss your mother,' she said. 'We haven't been apart for ten years. I'm going to miss her so much. Tell her I love her, Sam.'

Sam reached up and gave Velvet a face hug, hot tears slipping down her cheeks as Velvet shuddered. 'I'm so frightened,' Velvet said. 'I don't know what's going to happen to me.'

'We're getting you out of here, I promise,' Sam said.

'Sam?' said a soft voice on her right. Sam looked around and saw Lucy's black and white head hanging over the door of the stable next door. Sam reached out her hand and stroked her nose. 'I need Janey,' Lucy said, her voice full of anxiety.

'I know,' Sam said. 'You're going home tonight.'

'She can't be without me, Sam,' Lucy said. 'We're bonded. She'll cry and cry and cry and there will be no one there who can make her feel better.'

'Please let me go home too,' said another voice. A pretty little grey pony popped its head over the next stable door. 'My family will be missing me—I belong to three little boys.'

'I want my mummy,' said a little voice at the end of the stable block. Sam ran to it and looked over the door. A young foal was getting to its feet, all long legs and short lamb's tail. Its eyes were huge in its face.

'I want my mummy,' it said again, as it trotted over to the door and reached up to Sam with its nose. 'I'm so cold and hungry.'

There was a thud on her left and Sam whirled around in time to see Mulberry had jumped the fence. Luckily, a discarded stable rug had cushioned the sound of her hooves hitting concrete. She walked cautiously over to Sam, trying to keep her hoof beats as quiet as possible, while the Shetlands wriggled under the fence.

'You've been ages,' she hissed at Sam. 'What's the hold-up?'

'The stable doors are all padlocked,' Sam said. 'I can't get them open without a key.'

Mulberry looked at the doors and hissed with rage through her clenched teeth. She looked at Velvet, Lucy, and the little grey pony, and then she looked at Sam.

'We've got to get out of here, Sam,' she said.

'But we've only got tonight . . . ' Sam said.

'Maybe the thieves will get lazy and not move them on tomorrow, and give us time to think of something else,' Mulberry said. 'But I don't see how we are going to get those locks open tonight. We have to leave them and get you back to the yard.'

The little grey pony gasped in horror, while Lucy dropped her head in despair and the little foal whimpered. Velvet looked at Sam and nodded her head.

'She's right, Sam, go home. There is nothing you can do for us and I don't want you to get caught. These thieves are not nice people.'

'I can't just leave you!' Sam said.

106

'You can,' Velvet said. 'You must.'

'Let's go,' Mulberry said, while the Shetlands looked at each other.

'No, I'm not leaving them,' Sam said. 'There has to be something we can do.'

'Like what?' Mulberry asked.

'We're just going to have to call the police and admit that we are out here in the first place,' Sam said.

'Good idea,' Mulberry said. 'But we're going to have to leave the yard to do that. You can't be found here, Sam.'

'We can't leave them to be sold on to who knows where!' Sam said. 'Have a heart, Mulberry—there's a tiny foal here that isn't even old enough to be weaned. He'll starve.'

'I have a heart!' Mulberry snapped. 'But my job is to look after you.'

A tiny little cough came from somewhere near the floor at the end of the stable block and a small voice said, 'I think I can help. But only if you ask me nicely.'

Chapter 10

Sam walked to the end of the stable block and looked down. There was a hutch pushed back against the wall and the strangest-looking animal was sitting inside it, its eyes staring up at her. It had a very long body—so long that its back arched up in a curve like the Loch Ness monster. It had a long tail, short, stubby legs, and a narrow, snake-like head. It was covered in cream fur and it blinked narrow brown eyes at her. A musky smell drifted up to Sam's nostrils that she had never smelt before and a whistling snore was coming from the sleeping box in the hutch. The ponies crowded around, while the animal continued to stare up at them and say nothing.

'What is it?' Turbo asked.

Apricot took a deep, snuffling breath through her big nostrils. 'It's a weasel,' she said.

'I'm a ferret, actually,' said the little animal. 'Weasels are much smaller, much less intelligent, and much less useful than ferrets.'

'Whatever,' Apricot said. 'You look like a weasel.'

'You look like a baby hippo but you don't hear me getting personal, do you?' said the ferret.

Mulberry sniggered, while Apricot glared down at the hutch.

'You said you might be able to help?' Sam asked.

'No "might" about it—I can help,' said the ferret. 'But only on one condition.' Mulberry rolled her eyes. 'I saw that,' said the ferret.

'Oh, I'm sorry,' Mulberry said with mock innocence. 'Did I roll my eyes out loud?'

The ferret snorted. 'Oh no, I'm sorry,' said the little ferret with exaggerated politeness. 'I must have given you the impression I care what you think.'

The Shetlands sniggered. 'It's got a gob on it, I'll give it that,' Mickey said, while Mulberry narrowed her eyes at the ferret.

'I'm not an "it", I'm a "she",' said the ferret. She looked up at Sam. 'My name is Mindy.'

'Pleased to meet you,' Sam said. 'We really need to get these horses and ponies home. We would be very grateful if you can help.'

'I can, but you have to bring us along with you when you leave,' Mindy said.

'Who's "us"?' Mulberry asked.

'Me and my brother, Mike,' Mindy said.

'The one who is snoring his way through all this excitement.'

'Why do you want to come with us?' Sam asked.

'Look around,' Mindy said. 'Do these people look like animal lovers? This hutch is filthy all the time, the food is disgusting, and they don't change our water anywhere near enough. I don't get out much either and being cooped up in a tiny hutch is beginning to send me round the twist.'

'I don't know if my mum will let me bring you home, though,' Sam said.

'Doesn't matter,' Mindy said. 'We can live on your yard as long as we have got somewhere warm and dark to burrow and plenty of big, juicy rats to snack on.'

The ponies all looked disgusted and

Turbo said, 'I think I feel sick,' in a very faint voice.

'Meat eaters!' Mulberry said. 'You are revolting!'

Mindy sneered. 'I bet you don't like rats running around your stable or weeing all over your food though, do you? You vegetarians need us, whether you like it or not.'

'Look, I'm happy to bring you along with us,' Sam said, interrupting before a fight started. 'I don't like the thought of leaving any animal in this place, to be honest. But how can you help?'

'Easy,' Mindy said. 'All these padlocks were bought new when Her Majesty here made a run for it. The keys are all together on the same key ring, which is hanging up in the kitchen of the farmhouse. There's a cat flap in the kitchen door, so all I have to do is scoot in, climb up on the worktop, grab the keys, and run out here and give them to you. I can put the keys in your hand in five minutes.'

'A cat flap?' Apricot said. 'Does that mean there's a cat hanging around the place?' She looked at Mindy. 'Not exactly big, are you? How are you going to take on a fully grown cat?'

Mindy peeled back her lips in a humourless grin, her tiny white fangs gleaming in the moonlight. 'Don't you worry about that cat, she's got it coming.'

'I'm not even going to ask what that means,' Sam muttered as she undid the catches to the top of the hutch.

'Come on then, chop, chop,' Mulberry said. 'We don't have all night.'

'Hang on a sec,' Mindy said. 'I need backup.'

Her head and upper body disappeared into the sleeping compartment for a moment and then she backed out, dragging another ferret by the tail. He was twice the size of Mindy, with dark grey and brown fur on his body that formed a dramatic grey and cream mask on his face, like a raccoon, while his legs and paws were a glossy black. His whistling snore didn't

stop and his eyelids didn't so much as flicker, even when his chin bumped over the lip of the opening into the sleeping compartment and crashed down onto the floor of the hutch. Mindy looked down on him in disgust, while he continued to snore at her feet, blissfully unaware that he had been dragged out of his bed.

'What's wrong with him?' Turbo asked.

'Absolutely nothing,' Mindy said. 'I swear, if he didn't have to eat, he wouldn't wake up at all. That two-legs there could pick him up and swing him around her head and he still wouldn't wake up.'

Mulberry nudged Sam. 'Go on then,' she said, her eyes gleaming with delight.

'"Go on" what?' Sam asked.

'Swing him around your head,' Mulberry said. 'I want to see if he sleeps through it.' The Shetlands nodded while Mindy looked bored.

'I am not doing that!' Sam said, shocked. 'It's cruel!'

'But she said you could,' Apricot said, her face falling with disappointment. 'It's not cruel if you have the animal's permission, is it?'

Sam ignored them all and crouched down next to the hutch. 'We really are in a hurry. Could you wake him up without me having to swing him through the air?'

'No problem,' said Mindy, and, before

Sam could stop her, she sank her teeth into Mike's furry rump.

'Ouch!' Mike squealed, twisting his head round and raising his upper body off the floor to glare at Mindy. 'Whatcha do that for?'

'We're getting out of here, you lazy lump, so you need to get up!' Mindy hissed.

Mike yawned. His fangs were bigger than Mindy's but they didn't seem as scary on him, probably because he seemed less likely to use them than Mindy, who had a very cross expression on her face. He scratched at his belly with one paw. 'Where we going then?' he asked.

'To a new yard, with this lot,' Mindy said.

'But we've got to get the others free first.'

'You can't—we've got no keys,' Mike said. 'So if that means the move is off, I'm going back to bed.'

He started to climb back into the sleep compartment but Mindy grabbed his tail and pulled him back again.

'I know, you fur-brained fool, that's why we're going into the house to get them!' she said. 'I need you to look out for the cat.'

Mike groaned. 'Do we have to? It's going to be an awful lot of effort to get those keys and I can't be bothered. Can't we just stay here?'

'No,' Mindy said, ramming him with her head and forcing her brother over to the side of the hutch. 'Now get moving or I will bite your bum again.'

Mike sighed and stretched his long body against the wire mesh of the hutch wall. He was so long that, even with his back legs still on the ground, his front paws reached the top of the mesh frame and he pulled himself up and flowed over the side like furry water. Mindy quickly climbed over to join him on the ground, where he sat scratching behind an ear with one shiny black paw.

'Fine,' he said, jaws splitting wide in another huge yawn. 'I'll look out for the cat if you do all the leg work.'

'I always do,' Mindy grumbled, setting off across the yard towards the back door of the farmhouse with a funny, hopping run, her arched back making strange shadows on the ground. Mike yawned again and set off after her, at a much slower pace. Sam was worried he was falling asleep again already as he seemed to be leaning to one side as he ran. But within seconds both ferrets had vanished through the grubby white plastic cat flap inserted into the back door. Sam held her breath and strained her ears, listening for the sound of a cat discovering them in the kitchen—she had no doubt Mindy would put up quite a fight. But there was nothing but silence, broken by the foal's sobbing.

'Five minutes,' Mulberry warned. 'Then we're out of here.'

Sam crossed her fingers and waited.

Chapter 11

The seconds ticked past and still the yard stayed peaceful. There was no sound of a cat yowling or the clash and smash of pots and plates being hurled to the floor as cat and ferrets fought. Sam kept her eyes fixed on the cat flap—she didn't dare look around in case she had to see the hope and fear in Velvet's and Lucy's eyes. She couldn't bear to leave any of them behind. This had to work!

Mindy's little blonde head poked out of the cat flap and she trotted through the yard with her head held as high as she could so she wouldn't trip over the bunch

of keys held in her mouth. Mike ambled
along behind her. Sam went light-headed
with relief and excitement as she held her
hand out for those precious keys.

'Not so fast,' Mindy said, which isn't
easy to say when you have a key ring in
your mouth. 'You'll get the keys when I
know you're taking us with you.'

'How do I prove that?' Sam asked,
confused.

'Stuff us down your T-shirt, so you can't

leave us behind when you go,' Mike said. 'Besides, I need a nap.'

'She promised, didn't she?' Mulberry said, outraged. 'Sam wouldn't lie about something like that—she gave you her word.'

'No offence, but I don't know you,' Mindy said to Sam. 'Pick us up and then you get the keys.'

Sam bent down and scooped both ferrets up in her hands. Mindy was so small—not much bigger than a four-month-old kitten. Her bones felt as light and fragile as a bird's and her fur was soft and fine. Mike was much more solid and muscular and his coat thicker and coarser. Sam hesitated for a moment and then put both ferrets under her T-shirt, tucking the hem of it into the waistband of her jodhpurs so they wouldn't fall out. It felt weird as the little furry bodies squirmed against her tummy. Mike curled up for another nap, while Mindy pricked Sam's skin with her curved claws as she stretched up to poke her head through the neck of Sam's T-shirt with the keys.

'There you go,' she said, dropping them into Sam's outstretched palm. 'Told you we were useful.'

'Thank you,' Sam said, as Mindy pulled her head back into Sam's T-shirt and curled up next to her brother, who was snoring again already.

'Let's get out of here,' Mulberry said.

Sam turned to Velvet's door and fumbled with the keys. There was a different key for each of the four locks and she had to try two before the right one slid into the heavy brass padlock. She twisted it between trembling fingers, the lock turned with a tiny little snick sound, and the padlock opened. She worked the key off the ring and tossed both the padlock and the key into the dirt before muffling the iron bolt on Velvet's stable door with one hand and easing it open with the other. The bolt was old and rusty and didn't move as easily as the padlock. She wiggled the bolt up and down to ease it back millimetre by millimetre and it slowly moved back, creaking in protest. Sam was sweating with fear by the time the bolt was all the way back and she felt dizzy as she bent to gently turn the kick bolt over. Velvet nodded as Sam put a finger to her lips and swung the door wide. The big mare brushed past her, practically tiptoeing on hooves the size of dinner plates. Her coat was wet with sweat and it gleamed like a mirror in the moonlight. Sam breathed a small sigh of relief.

'Your turn,' she whispered to Lucy, who nodded eagerly. Again, Sam searched for the right key, and gently eased the rusty bolt open. With Lucy free, she moved on to the next stable. The little grey pony rolled his huge dark eyes in panic and his breathing came in shallow gasps, his large nostrils flaring as he panted.

'Please don't leave me!' he said in a terrified whinny.

'Ssssh!' said Mulberry and the Shetlands as Sam put her hand on his hot nose.

'We're not going to leave anyone behind,' Sam whispered. 'But you've got to be really, really quiet.'

'I've got children waiting for me,' the little pony said, who didn't seem to hear what Sam had said. 'They will be so worried, they will be crying. I've never left home before, not for a whole night.'

'I know, I know,' Sam said. 'But please be quiet or you're going to get us caught.'

'Don't bother talking, Sam, just get him out,' Apricot said. 'A panicking pony ain't listening to anyone. Get him out of that stable and he'll calm down quick enough, otherwise he'll get us rumbled.'

'Oh, that's already happened,' said a silky voice behind Sam. She whirled around and saw a silver tabby cat perched on a

rain barrel. Her green eyes glowed in the moonlight and her tail lashed from side to side in anger. 'The horse has already bolted on that one, if you pardon the pun. How did you get those keys, little two-legs?' She sniffed at the air and then looked at the hutch. 'Ah, I should have known.' Her mouth curled with contempt. 'Betrayed by two sneaky little weasels.'

'Ferrets!' squeaked Mindy from somewhere around Sam's stomach.

Sam licked her lips with a tongue that felt as dry as sandpaper as she tried to find enough spit to speak with. 'These horses and ponies have been stolen—they have loving owners who need to get them home,' Sam said. 'That little foal needs to be with his mum. You wouldn't like to be taken away, would you?'

The tabby cat unsheathed one long, wicked-looking paw, and dragged deep scratches through the wood of the rain barrel. 'I don't really care where I am, as long as I have food and a comfy place to sleep. I get all that here. And, unlike those two little weasels you seem to have stuffed down your T-shirt, I don't bite the hand that feeds me. So if I were you, I'd put those horses back where you found them.'

Behind Sam, the little grey pony began to rock from hoof to hoof, weaving his head with distress. Mulberry shook her mane.

'We're all going home, fleabag,' she said. 'Whether you like it or not.'

The cat lidded her emerald eyes and purred. 'Now, now, there really is no need to be rude. The fact is, I *don't* like it and I *can* do something about it.'

'Sam, get those last locks undone, quick smart,' Apricot said.

'Don't you move, you runt,' hissed the cat, arching her back and spitting with temper, every hair on her body standing on end.

Sam froze, her wide eyes fixed on the cat. She knew she had to move fast but she was transfixed by the cat's baleful stare and the fear of what she could do. The feel of Mindy's long body wriggling against her chest as the ferret hooked her claws into the cotton of Sam's T-shirt to climb up again and whisper in Sam's ear broke the spell.

'Do it!' hissed the ferret. 'She's going to wake the whole place up anyway, the spiteful thing!'

Sam started to shake uncontrollably as she turned back to the grey pony and put a key in the lock. It only went halfway in before it got stuck. It was the wrong one. Behind her, the cat gave a low yowl and she looked over her shoulder. There was a metal bucket next to the rain barrel that Sam hadn't noticed and even as she saw it, the cat jumped off the rain barrel and aimed all four paws at the bucket. The force of her impact knocked the bucket onto its side where it made a loud clang on the concrete. The cat reared up and batted at it, sending it rolling across the yard. The cat looked at Sam and then opened her mouth and let out the most hair-raising screech Sam had ever heard.

'They're getting away, they're getting away!' yowled the tabby, her eyes gleaming with malice.

The grey pony lost what little self-control he had been hanging onto and began to neigh in desperation, letting out a panic-stricken shrick that sounded closer to a train whistle than something that could come out of an animal's throat. Velvet and Lucy reared in terror as they heard a shout come from the house and a light was switched on in one of the upstairs rooms.

Sam looked up as the yellow electric light flooded her face and she saw curtains twitch. A man was looking down at her with a very angry expression on his face, thick black hair sticking up all over his head. His jaw dropped in disbelief when he saw her and then he saw Velvet and Lucy. He started to bang on the window and shout.

'Now it really is time to go,' Mulberry said.

Chapter 12

I can do this, thought Sam, as she turned back to the grey pony's stable and the big shiny padlock that was still trapping him inside. His eyes were blank with fear and she had to crouch to avoid him hitting her with his head as he swung it from side to side. Her fingers were slick with sweat and she nearly started to cry when the last two keys slid from her hand and bounced off the ground.

'We've got go, Sam,' urged Mulberry as Sam groped about for the keys. 'We've got to get you out of here.'

'There're only two locks left,' Sam said,

as the cat continued to yowl and shriek behind her and more lights came on in the house. 'It will take seconds to get them open.' Her grasping fingers found the keys and she picked one and slipped it into the lock. It got stuck halfway and wouldn't move any further. Sam had picked the wrong key again. Something loomed up behind her and blocked her light. Sam screamed before she realized it was Velvet.

'Mulberry's right,' said the big black mare, her eyes rolling with fear. 'We have to go now—there is nothing else you can do!' She reached down and took some of Sam's T-shirt between her teeth and tried to pull her away but Sam shrugged her off as the second key slid home in the lock. She pulled the bolt back and the little pony nearly knocked her flying as he shot out of the stable like a cork from a bottle, colliding with Velvet. The sound of booted feet thundering down uncarpeted stairs came from the house and the kitchen light blinked on.

'Go on, Sam!' Apricot yelled. 'We've got your back!'

Sam shoved the last key into the last lock and unbolted the last door. But the little foal didn't come racing out, slipping and sliding on the concrete as his long baby legs struggled to keep up. Instead, he had backed into a corner at the far end of the stable and his tiny body shook with fear. Sam stepped into the stable.

'It's OK,' she said, holding out a hand that was shaking as much as the foal. 'I'm not going to hurt you, I'm going to get you home to your mum.'

But the terrified foal whimpered and didn't move.

'What is going on out here?' shouted a rough voice. Sam crouched down on the floor of the stable. 'Where did all these blasted Shetlands come from?!'

'There's a kid with them,' said another voice, just as rough and nasty as the first. 'I saw it.'

'Oh, is there?' said the first voice. 'Well, you're in big trouble, kid. But we won't be angry if you come out now and stop hiding. All these animals can go back into their stables and there's no harm done. But if you make us come looking for you . . . ' The voice trailed off, the cat stopped yowling, the grey pony stopped panicking, and the threat was heavy in the silence.

Sam clapped her hand over her mouth

to stop herself from making a noise. Then she heard the tap, tap, tap of hooves.

'Don't you worry, Sam,' Mulberry said, her flat, menacing tone drifting into the stable. 'These idiots are not going to get to so much as breathe near you.'

'Is that what I think it is?' said the second voice.

'Well, I'll be—!' said the first voice, letting out a low whistle of amazement. 'That's the one that ran off on us. How did you find your way back here, eh? No matter, you horrible little devil, we're going to lock you up proper this time.'

Sam heard one of the thieves take a slow, careful step towards Mulberry, who started to paw at the ground in temper. That was a sure sign Mulberry was about to charge, teeth bared. Sam held her breath, but

before Mulberry and the thieves collided, Sam heard Apricot shout, 'Skittles!'

Sam swivelled on her heels and peeked over the half-open stable door just in time to see Apricot, Mickey, and Turbo charge at the two thieves. Their round little bodies were so low to the ground that the thieves couldn't grab at them to push them back as the Shetlands collided with their legs and knocked them onto their backs. Once they had them down on the ground the Shetlands grabbed mouthfuls of clothing and shook the men hard.

Turbo bit one on the leg. 'That's for taking friends from my herd!' he said.

Mickey kicked the other on the bum. 'That's for taking a little foal!' he said.

Apricot headbutted him in the chest when he tried to get to his feet. 'That's for everyone here and all the ponies you've ever stolen, you horrible, scummy two-legs!'

Sam felt the prick of tiny claws again against her chest and Mindy nuzzled her ear, her little fangs hard against her earlobe. 'This would be an ideal moment to make our getaway,' she said. 'So get moving or do I have to give you a good, hard nip as well?'

Velvet's head popped over the stable door and she whinnied gently to the little foal. 'Come along, little one, your mother is waiting for you,' she said, her warm, rich voice filling the stable, as comforting as a hug. Sam went weak with relief—the big mare seemed to have calmed down and was back in charge.

'Do you know where my mummy is?'

the foal asked in a tiny voice, his scrawny, ribby little body still trembling.

'I do, little one,' Velvet said. 'We're all going to leave right now and we're going to go to a nice, safe place where your mummy will find you. But you've got to come with me, right now, or the bad men will lock us up again.'

The foal looked at Sam. 'Is that two-legs going to hurt me?' he asked Velvet.

Velvet shook her head. 'She's not going to hurt a hair on your little head,' she said. 'She came here to help us all go home.'

'OK,' said the little foal, and, very cautiously, he put one tiny hoof in front of the other until he had managed to get halfway across the stable, and then he ran for the door, curling his body away from Sam.

Mindy nipped at Sam's ear. 'No excuses, move!'

Outside, the two thieves were still being rolled around on the concrete by the Shetlands, who seemed to be doing their best to tenderize them. The commotion had kicked up a cloud of dust and the thieves coughed and spluttered. The silver tabby had climbed into the guttering and was glaring down at an angry Mulberry. The mare's eyes were slits of boiling black rage and she stretched her neck and snapped her teeth at the cat who remained just out of range.

'Get down here, you spiteful little wretch,' she hissed. 'Get down here and I'll show you what we do to animals who put two-legs first, you little traitor.'

'I'm not the one who lets them strap me up in leather, stick a bit in my mouth, and ride me wherever they want me to go,' said the cat. 'You ponies are all the same: weak-minded, servile, pathetic—you're as bad as dogs!'

'Come down here and say that!' roared Mulberry.

The cat sniggered and shook her head. 'I'm not as stupid as you—the pony who didn't even notice she was walking onto a horse lorry!'

Mulberry reared up and snapped her teeth dangerously close to the cat's thick fur. The cat screeched and leapt past Mulberry onto the ground, tearing off in a silvery streak around the corner of the house, and was gone. Mulberry stamped her hoof with annoyance and then she spotted Sam and trotted over.

'Hop on, young 'un, and let's get out of this miserable place,' she whinnied.

'Couldn't have put it better myself,' Mindy said, while Mike turned over against Sam's stomach and said, 'Wha'? Wazza matter? Where we goin'?'

Sam grabbed a handful of Mulberry's mane and sprang up onto her back. The little mare snorted, half reared, and then charged forward into the night so fast Sam was convinced she had left her shadow behind. 'Hold on tight!' she yelled to Mindy, who dug her claws into Sam's stomach. Mike snored on, rolling against Sam's T-shirt, which, thankfully, was still tucked snugly into her jodhpurs. It was about the only thing stopping the lazy ferret from falling out and tumbling to the ground. She heard Mindy give a terrified squeak as Sam folded over Mulberry's neck as she leapt to clear the fence. Sam began to slide forward as Mulberry landed and galloped off, unable to grip the mare's sleek sides with her legs.

'Mulberry, I'm going to fall!' she screamed, full of terror as the wind rushed past her ears. Mulberry slowed to a canter and shrugged her big shoulders, pushing Sam back.

'No, you're not!' she said. 'I NEVER drop you, Sam.'

Up ahead, Sam could see Velvet and Lucy cantering slowly, the little foal between them, running as fast as his spindly legs would go, the little grey pony following in their tracks like a wisp of cloud. She looked over her shoulder but that horrible

yard was already being swallowed by the summer night.

'What about the Shetlands?' she yelled in Mulberry's ear over the wind.

'They'll be fine—they'll catch us up,' Mulberry yelled back. 'Fair play to them, they were right about those hidden skills. Who knew the baby hippos would be so handy in a fight?'

Sam laughed as Mulberry ran on and, sure enough, a few minutes later, she looked over her shoulder and she could see familiar little barrel-shaped ponies galloping after them, their stubby legs a blur.

'Mulberry, wait, they are trying to catch up!' Sam yelled.

Mulberry slowed to a trot as Mickey, Turbo, and Apricot ran up to them.

'Did you see us?' asked fat little Turbo, his eyes sparkling with excitement. 'Did you see?'

'I did,' Sam giggled. 'You were amazing, Tub Tubs. But I hope you didn't hurt them too badly?'

Mickey snorted. 'They are going to have a lot of big bruises and they might have a bit of a limp in the morning, but that's about it.'

'No more than they deserve,' Mulberry said.

'Just as well we came along, eh?' Apricot said. 'You'd have been finished without us.'

'I'd have managed,' Mulberry said.

'Yeah, right,' Apricot snorted. 'It just goes to show, if you want a job done properly, get a Shetland to do it.'

Sam smiled happily and began to relax as they trotted home, the familiar sound of Apricot and Mulberry bickering fading into background noise. Up ahead, Velvet's and Lucy's big bums swayed from side to side, their thick, rippling tails bouncing as they went. The foal was safely tucked away between them, his lamb's tail flicking up and down with joy. The little grey pony was shaking his head and snorting with relief as his neat little hooves trotted along smartly. Mindy took her claws out of Sam's stomach and snuggled down next to her brother for the journey to their new home.

Chapter 13

They retraced their footsteps home, striking out across the dark countryside where the thieves would find it impossible to follow them on foot without a light to guide them and over terrain too rough and awkward for a car. As deep as country people slept before they faced another working day, it would be hard to sleep through the sound of a 4 x 4 struggling to break through hedgerows to follow the tracks of the horses and ponies. The night grew darker as the dawn approached but Sam could dimly make out every horse and pony swivelling its ears backwards

and forwards to try and hear if they were being followed. Sam knew that equine hearing was much, much better than a human's and that any of them would know, long before she heard anything, if the thieves were coming. But they all trotted steadily on, their breathing soft and rhythmic in the night, all signs of panic and anger fading. It was so peaceful that Sam found herself nodding off on Mulberry's back. The last two days had been very emotional and Sam was exhausted. She couldn't wait to lie down in Miss Mildew's rock-hard guest bed and force her limbs between those sheets that seemed to have a stranglehold on the mattress. In fact, Sam was so tired that even if the only bed offered to her once they got back to Meadow Vale was a box full of gravel she would still stretch on it and fall fast asleep.

She tried to stay awake as she didn't want to slither off Mulberry's back in her sleep and hurt the ferrets. They were a warm weight against her belly, their fur kitten-soft. She yawned and blinked and opened her eyes as wide as they could go in an effort to stay awake. But her head kept lolling on her neck and her heavy eyelids kept trying to close. The countryside was passing in sleep-fogged blur.

'Wake up, Sam, we're home,' Mulberry said.

Sam jerked awake with a start. She had dozed off after all and, even worse, she had been drooling. Embarrassed, she wiped at her mouth with her hand. Turbo was looking up at her with his bright black eyes.

'You snore,' he said.

'I do not!' Sam said.

'Do too!' sang Apricot and Mickey.

'Do I?' she asked Mulberry.

'Yep,' said the little mare. 'Like a pig with asthma.'

'Let's get to our stables,' Velvet said. 'It will be dawn soon and this little one needs to rest.' Sam looked down at the little foal who was yawning and swaying from side to side with tiredness.

'Do I get to see Janey now?' Lucy asked.

'Soon,' Sam promised. 'But you'll have to wait for a couple of hours. I need to get myself back into bed so it looks like I never left the yard at all. It has to look like you guys found your way home, just like Mulberry. Too many questions are going to get asked otherwise.'

'But I really need to see her,' Lucy said.

'I want to see my rider too,' Velvet said gently. 'But we can't get Sam into trouble, not after she put herself in danger to come and get us.'

'Sam was never in danger,' Mulberry said, with an edge to her voice. She didn't like it if she thought Velvet was ever criticizing how she looked after Sam. 'She's always safe when she is with me.'

'Let's get home,' Sam said. She really didn't want an argument between her two favourite animals in the world. She squeezed her legs in a signal to walk on and Mulberry was so well trained she didn't even think about it. Off she went, with everyone else trailing in her wake.

Sam slid down from her back at the end of the driveway.

'I don't think you should go back in your stables—we'll make too much noise,' she whispered to Velvet and Lucy. 'It will look too strange as well. It's a nice night and the yard will be up soon, so why don't you sleep in the field until everyone gets here for work?'

Lucy yawned. 'Right now, I think I would sleep on the compost heap.'

'I can't go another step,' Velvet agreed. 'I'll lie anywhere, just as long as I can sleep.'

'And then I'll get to go home?' asked the little grey pony.

'Yes, I promise,' Sam said.

'OK then.'

So Sam led them to the fields that stretched out on the hill that rose above the yard and quietly opened the five-bar gate into a lush summer meadow filled with soft springy grass and wild flowers. It was an hour before the dawn, when the night is darkest, and Sam couldn't really see but she could hear Velvet and Lucy sink to their knees with a groan of relief.

'Lie next to me, little one, and keep warm,' Velvet called softly to the foal. 'Your mother will be here soon.' The little foal was too exhausted to argue and collapsed in a tangle of limbs against Velvet's dark bulk. The little grey pony flopped out on the grass and was asleep as soon as his head touched the ground. Sam crept forward and put a hand on Velvet's and Lucy's heads in turn as they lowered them to the ground.

'Night, night, sleep tight,' she whispered.
'See you in a couple of hours.'

All she got in reply was soft snores.

Mulberry was waiting for her on the
driveway when Sam walked back down
from the fields. The Shetlands had already
squeezed back under the gate and were
snoring loudly in the barn, snuggled down
in soft, thick beds of hay. Mulberry yawned
as they walked quietly to her stable.

'That was a good night's work, two-legs,'
she said. 'You can be proud of what you've
done tonight.'

Sam smiled as she let Mulberry back
into her stable. 'I couldn't have done it
without you, you know.'

'Course you couldn't,' Mulberry said. 'I was just trying to be gracious.'

'We do make a good team, don't we?' Sam asked.

Mulberry nuzzled her cheek. 'The best,' she said, yawning another huge yawn. 'Now get to bed, young 'un, before you get caught wandering around the yard and everyone finds out exactly what you've been doing.'

Sam kissed Mulberry on the nose and tiptoed around the stable block, then crouched down and crawled over to the sash window she had left open in what seemed like another lifetime.

Both the ferrets were still snoring gently and she cradled them in her arms through her T-shirt. She didn't really know what to do with them but it didn't seem right to simply shake them out onto the ground and let them find a bed for themselves. So she climbed back into the bedroom, eased them out from under her T-shirt and pushed their warm, furry bodies under the sheets and blankets. She quickly changed into her pyjamas and slipped into bed. She felt Mike and Mindy stir in their sleep and snuggle closer to her leg. She fluffed up her pillow, pulled the blankets up to her chin, and yawned. She was fast asleep in seconds.

Chapter 14

'**W**ake up, Miss Grey, it seems the excitement is never-ending around here!'

Sam cracked open an eyelid. Miss Mildew was throwing open the curtains to the bedroom and the early morning sunshine hammered into Sam's tired eyes.

'Huh?' she said, her tongue thick in her head.

'It would appear that miracles do happen and our lost sheep are returned to us,' Miss Mildew said.

'But you don't keep sheep, Miss Mildew,' Sam muttered, her brain failing to wake up as fast as the rest of her.

Miss Mildew tutted. 'It seems that anything but the plainest of language is wasted on you, Miss Grey,' Miss Mildew said. She leaned down and spoke slowly and loudly, as if Sam were hard of hearing. 'Velvet and Lucy have come home and it seems they have brought a couple of waifs and strays with them. Up, up—your mother is on her way.' Miss Mildew was about to sweep out of the room when she paused at the door and turned, sniffing at the air. 'What is that smell?'

Sam froze and buried herself under the blankets again to hide the blush that was heating her cheeks. 'I don't know what you mean, Miss Mildew. I can't smell anything strange.'

'It smells like . . . ' began Miss Mildew.

'Never mind. Up and dressed, Miss Grey—we have a busy day ahead.'

Sam sighed with relief as Miss Mildew closed the door behind her and she felt two warm, long, furry bundles move up from the bottom of the bed. Mindy popped her head out from under the sheets.

'Cheek! Who is she calling smelly?' the little blonde ferret asked. 'She doesn't smell too good to me neither, but you don't hear me complaining.'

Mike stuck his head out next and yawned. 'When's breakfast?'

'I have no idea,' Sam said, picking them up and walking over to the

169

window. 'You're going to have to sort yourselves out this morning.' She opened the window with one hand, leaned out, and carefully put them down in the garden. 'This is your new home so go off and explore. I'll look for you later.'

'At least find us some lunch,' Mike said.

'I'll see what I can do,' Sam said. 'Now go!'

The ferrets gave themselves a good shake and ran off with their funny, hopping run. Sam ducked back into the room and started to get dressed, dizzy with tiredness. She was so happy for Mum and Janey but she would have given anything to be able to crawl back into bed and sleep for a few hours. But that would have looked too suspicious so Sam resigned herself to a long day and went to get some breakfast.

All her tiredness disappeared into the bright blue sky when she saw Mum's face. Sam walked onto the top yard to find her mother in Velvet's stable, sobbing into Velvet's mane, her face alight with joy.

'Oh, my beautiful girl,' Mum wept. 'I thought I would never see you again.' Velvet wrapped her long neck around Mum and held her close, rumbling deep in her throat, over and over again, nuzzling at Mum with her soft nose and licking every bit of bare skin she could find with her big pink tongue.

'Sam!' Mum said, when she looked up and saw Sam watching from the doorway. She held out her hand. 'We got her back— our family is whole again.' Sam rushed into her mother's hug and was swept up against Velvet's chest. She threw her arms out and clung on, to her mother and the horse that had been there her whole life, and breathed in the smell of them: the rich, spicy tang of Velvet, the chocolatey smell of Mum. Amy appeared at the door and slipped under Mum's arm for a group hug. Mum gave them all a hard squeeze and said, 'Now I have just about everyone I love, right here.'

She stood back and wiped at her eyes. 'All we need now is Dad and Mulberry, but I think she would start a fight,' Mum laughed.

The foal's mother was found quickly. His owners had put posters up everywhere with their number on it, desperate for his return. They arrived mid-morning with a horse trailer, his mother calling frantically as soon as they turned into the yard. Miss

Mildew let mother and foal settle down in one of her stables and the foal immediately started to suckle. Everyone agreed it would be too traumatic to move them again, so they were to stay at Meadow Vale until the little foal was well rested and a bit stronger.

A few phone calls found the little grey pony's family. A small red car came up the driveway at lunchtime and, sure enough,

three very excitable little boys came tumbling out of it, hugging and kissing the little pony who just shivered all over with delight, pawing the ground, whinnying and nuzzling each child in turn. They didn't have a trailer so Miss Mildew offered to drive the pony home using her own.

'Anything to get them off the yard,' Sam heard her grumble. 'The racket those boys make is dreadful.'

Sam realized she hadn't seen Janey or Lucy all day. Shortly after lunch, she walked down to Lucy's stable and looked over the door. Lucy was lying down in the straw, her legs tucked underneath her. Her long neck was stretched out and her head was in Janey's lap. Janey was sitting with her legs straight out in front of her, her arms around Lucy's neck, her head lolling against her shoulder. The two of them were fast asleep. Janey's face, although tear-stained, looked happy in her sleep. Sam tiptoed away and left them in peace.

Mulberry was awake and munching on a hay net when Sam went to see her.

'It's been quite a day, hasn't it, two-legs?' she said.

'It's been a long day,' Sam sighed. 'I am so tired and it's not even dinner time yet. But I am so glad everyone is home—it was worth it. Have you seen Mike and Mindy?'

'No, but I can smell them,' Mulberry said. 'I'd better see fewer rats round here if I'm going to be expected to put up with those two.'

Sam thought for a second as Mulberry munched. 'I was never in any real danger, was I?'

Mulberry snorted. 'Not the tiniest bit,' she said. 'As if I'd let anyone near you.'

Sam smiled and rubbed Mulberry's nose. 'Are you my gorgeous girl?'

'Could you be any more patronizing? But yes, I am gorgeous,' Mulberry said. 'I also think I've proved that I am brave and resourceful to boot, so I think that deserves as least one green apple, don't you?'

'I'm feeling generous,' Sam said. 'How about two green apples?'

'That's my girl,' Mulberry said, nuzzling Sam's cheek.

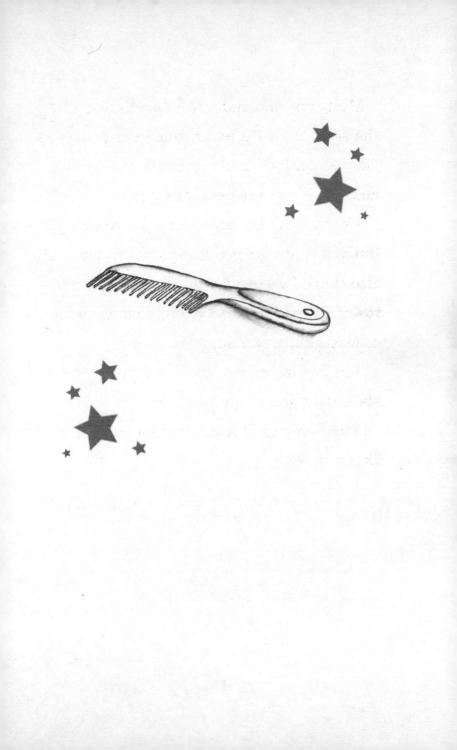

MEET THE PONIES!

Mulberry

BREED: Exmoor X Welsh. Both Welsh and Exmoor ponies are native British breeds. Both breeds are renowned for being intelligent, which Mulberry definitely is—and she knows it, too! Welsh ponies are often very spirited and lively, like Mulberry, whereas Exmoor ponies tend to have kinder and gentler temperaments. Both breeds are very strong despite their small size, and are tough enough to live outside all year round.

HEIGHT: 12.2hh (a 'hand' is 4 inches. So Mulberry is 12 and a half hands high.)

COLOUR: Jet black   **MARKINGS:** None

FAVOURITE FOOD: Pony nuts and fresh green apples.

LIKES: Sam, going fast, and being scratched behind the ears.

DISLIKES: Rain, bruised apples, and annoying Shetland ponies.

Velvet

BREED: Irish cob. Irish cobs are very sure-footed—making them really safe and comfortable to ride. They're exceptionally kind, very intelligent, and are big and strong, just like Velvet. Perfect for cuddles!

HEIGHT: 15.2hh

COLOUR: Black

MARKINGS: White star in between her eyes that looks like a big diamond.

FAVOURITE FOOD: Any treats, but especially carrots.

LIKES: Hugs, hay, and being taken out for rides.

DISLIKES: Naughty little ponies.

Apricot

BREED: Miniature Shetland pony. Shetland ponies originally come from the Shetland Islands in the very north of Scotland, although they're now found all over the world. Although they're the smallest native British breed, they're also the strongest (for their size). They are really brave, and tend to have very strong characters—which explains Apricot's feisty personality!

HEIGHT: 9hh

COLOUR: Dun with flaxen mane and tail. Dun is a warm shade of brown—like the colour of an apricot, and having a flaxen mane and tail is like having blonde hair.

MARKINGS: None

FAVOURITE FOOD: Hay, and lots of it!

LIKES: Making mischief and getting away with it!

DISLIKES: When Basil comes too close to the fence.

PARTS OF A PONY'S TACK
BRIDLE

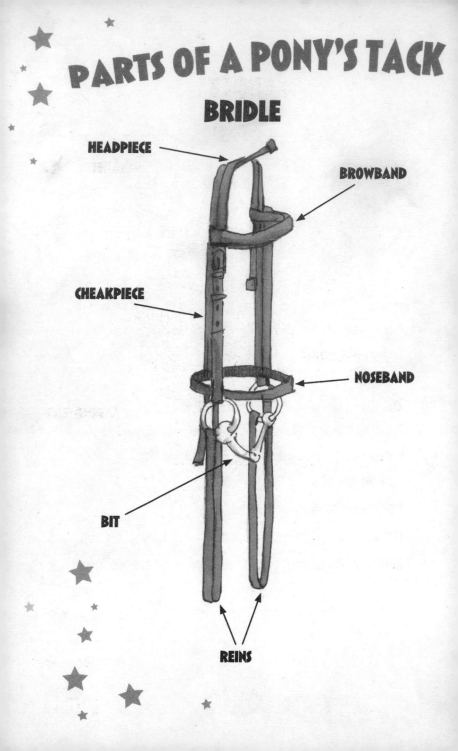

HEADPIECE

BROWBAND

CHEAKPIECE

NOSEBAND

BIT

REINS

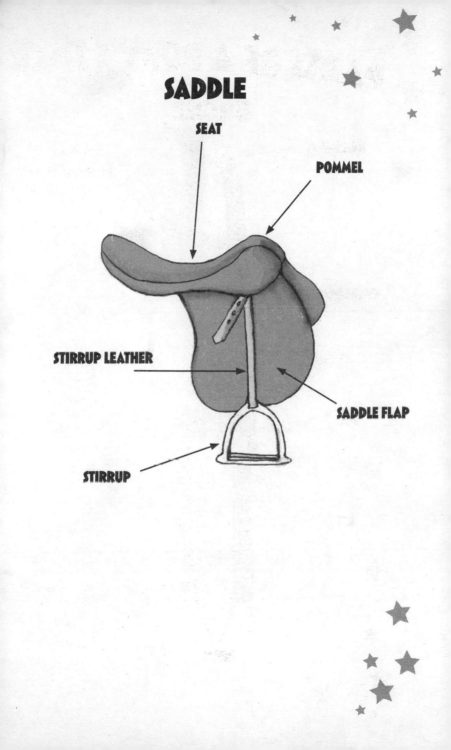

SADDLE

SEAT

POMMEL

STIRRUP LEATHER

SADDLE FLAP

STIRRUP

ABOUT THE AUTHOR!

CHE GOLDEN is a graduate of the Masters course in Creative Writing for Young People at Bath Spa University. *The Meadow Vale Ponies* series are her first books for Oxford University Press.

Che's first horse was Velvet, a huge, black Irish cob who not only taught Che how to ride, but taught her two little girls as well. Now, they own Charlie Brown, a rather neurotic New Forest pony, and Robbie, a very laid-back Highland pony. Mulberry is based on a little black mare, Brie, who Che's daughter fell in love with, despite the fact that Brie managed to terrorize a yard of 50 horses and vets wanted danger money to go anywhere near her.

Che also has two pet ferrets, Mike and Mindy, and a Manchester Terrier called Beau Nash.

Have you read MULBERRY'S other adventures?

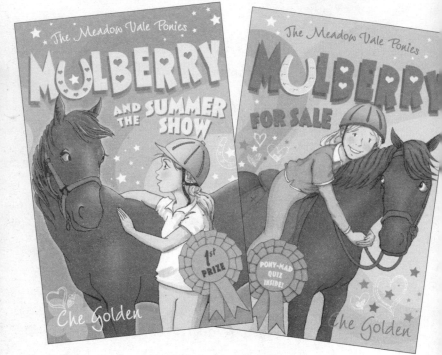